A Note to Parents and Caregivers:

Read-it! Readers are for children who are just starting on the amazing road to reading. These beautiful books support both the acquisition of reading skills and the love of books.

The RED LEVEL presents familiar topics using common words and repeating sentence patterns.

The BLUE LEVEL presents new ideas using a larger vocabulary and varied sentence structure.

The YELLOW LEVEL presents more challenging ideas, a broad vocabulary, and wide variety in sentence structure.

The GREEN LEVEL presents more complex ideas, an extended vocabulary range, and expanded language structures.

When sharing a book with your child, read in short stretches, pausing often to talk about the pictures. Have your child turn the pages and point to the pictures and familiar words. And be sure to reread favorite stories or parts of stories.

There is no right or wrong way to share books with children. Find time to read with your child, and pass on the legacy of literacy.

Adria F. Klein, Ph.D.
Professor Emeritus
California State University
San Bernardino, California

Managing Editor: Bob Temple
Creative Director: Terri Foley
Editor: Brenda Haugen
Editorial Adviser: Andrea Cascardi
Copy Editor: Laurie Kahn
Designer: Melissa Voda
Page production: The Design Lab
The illustrations in this book were prepared digitally.

Picture Window Books
5115 Excelsior Boulevard
Suite 232
Minneapolis, MN 55416
1-877-845-8392
www.picturewindowbooks.com

Printed in the United States of America.

Library of Congress Cataloging-in-Publication Data
Blair, Eric.
The dog and the wolf : a retelling of Aesop's fable / by Eric Blair ; illustrated by Dianne
Silverman.
p. cm. — (Read-it! readers)
Summary: After meeting a well-fed dog, a half-starved wolf is ready to exchange his life in
the wild for the daily comforts of food and shelter until he learns that a full belly is not
worth the price of freedom.
ISBN 1-4048-0323-8 (Reinforced Library Binding)
[1. Fables. 2. Folklore.] I. Aesop. II. Silverman, Dianne, ill. III.
Title. IV. Series.
PZ8.2.B595 Dl 2004
398.2—dc22
                                                                        2003016673

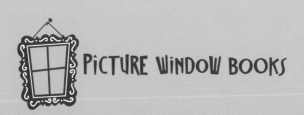

PICTURE WINDOW BOOKS

The Dog and the Wolf

A Retelling of Aesop's Fable
By Eric Blair

Illustrated by Dianne Silverman

Content Adviser:
Kathy Baxter, M.A.
Former Coordinator of Children's Services
Anoka County (Minnesota) Library

Reading Advisers:
Adria F. Klein, Ph.D.
Professor Emeritus, California State University
San Bernardino, California

Susan Kesselring, M.A.
Literacy Educator
Rosemount-Apple Valley-Eagan (Minnesota) School District

Picture Window Books
Minneapolis, Minnesota

What Is a Fable?

A fable is a story that teaches a lesson. In some fables, animals may talk and act the way people do. A Greek slave named Aesop created some of the world's favorite fables. Aesop's fables have been enjoyed by readers for more than 2,000 years.

One moonlit night, a starving wolf wandered alone through the countryside.

As he roamed the country, the skinny wolf met a well-fed dog.

"How is it that you look so sleek and happy, while I must go hungry?" asked the wolf.

"Cousin wolf, that's easy," answered
the dog. "What you need is a steady job.

Come with me, and help me guard my master's house. Then you'll have plenty to eat."

The hungry wolf gladly agreed.
He and the dog set off toward
the house.

On the way, the wolf noticed a strange mark on the dog's neck. "What is that?" asked the wolf.

"Nothing much," answered the dog.
"Perhaps the collar attached to my
chain was too tight."

"You mean you are not free to come and go as you please?" asked the wolf.

"Not exactly," answered the dog.

"During the day, my master ties me up," the dog explained. "But I'm a great favorite. My master and his servants feed me well."

"Farewell and good night," said the wolf.
"I'll have none of that. I'd rather
be free than full."

Levels for *Read-it!* Readers

Read-it! Readers help children practice early reading skills
with brightly illustrated stories.

Red Level: Familiar topics with frequently used words and repeating patterns.

Blue Level: New ideas with a larger vocabulary and a variety of language structures.

The Donkey in the Lion's Skin, by Eric Blair 1-4048-0320-3

The Goose that Laid the Golden Egg, by Mark White 1-4048-0219-3

Yellow Level: Challenging ideas with an expanded vocabulary and a wide variety of sentences.

The Ant and the Grasshopper, by Mark White 1-4048-0217-7

The Boy Who Cried Wolf, by Eric Blair 1-4048-0319-X

The Country Mouse and the City Mouse, by Eric Blair 1-4048-0318-1

The Crow and the Pitcher, by Eric Blair 1-4048-0322-X

The Dog and the Wolf, by Eric Blair 1-4048-0323-8

The Fox and the Grapes, by Mark White 1-4048-0218-5

The Tortoise and the Hare, by Mark White 1-4048-0215-0

The Wolf in Sheep's Clothing, by Mark White 1-4048-0220-7

Green Level: More complex ideas with an extended vocabulary range and expanded language structures.

Belling the Cat, by Eric Blair 1-4048-0321-1

The Lion and the Mouse, by Mark White 1-4048-0216-9